Good-bye Pony

Do you love ponies? Be a Pony Pal!

PONY PALS®

Good-bye Pony

Jeanne Betancourt

illustrated by Paul Bachem

A
LITTLE APPLE
PAPERBACK

SCHOLASTIC INC.
New York Toronto London Auckland Sydney

Thank you to Maria Genovesi and Dr. Kent Kay for sharing their knowledge of horses with me.

ISBN 0-590-54339-3

Text copyright © 1995 by Jeanne Betancourt.
Illustrations copyright © 1995 by Scholastic Inc.
All rights reserved. Published by Scholastic Inc.
APPLE PAPERBACKS® and the APPLE PAPERBACKS® logo are registered trademarks of Scholastic Inc.

12 11 10 9 8 7 6 5   7 8 9/9 0 1/0

Printed in the U.S.A.   40

First Scholastic printing, January 1996

Contents

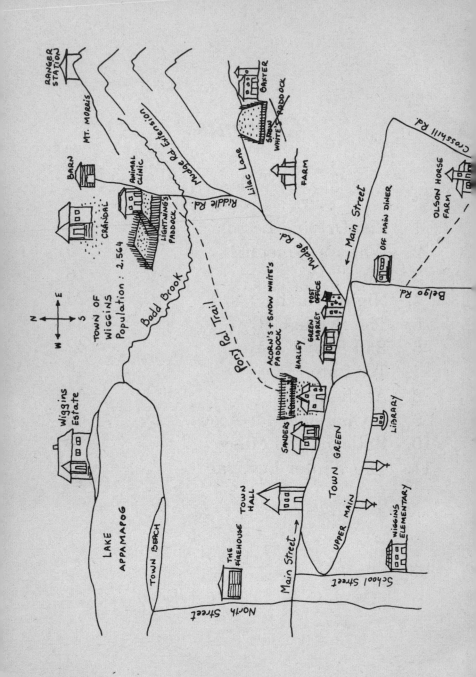

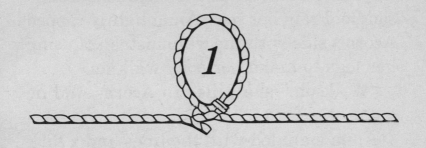

The Driving Lesson

Anna Harley sat in the cart behind her pony, Acorn. She was holding Acorn with extra-long reins called lines. Ms. Wiggins sat in the cart next to Anna. Acorn and Anna were learning carriage driving from Ms. Wiggins.

Ms. Wiggins' old pony, Winston, was watching the driving lesson from the paddock next to the Wiggins riding ring.

Anna was getting used to holding Acorn by the lines instead of shorter reins. Giving directions to a pony from a carriage was very different from giving directions from a saddle. From her seat, Anna lightly tapped Acorn's side with the whip instead of using her legs to make her pony walk on.

"Walk on," she called to Acorn. And he did.

Anna signaled with the lines and a flick of the whip for Acorn to turn left at the corner of the riding ring. Acorn made the turn then stopped in his tracks.

"Walk on," Anna called to her pony. Instead of moving forward, Acorn took two steps backward.

"Because of the blinders, he can't see Winston," Anna told Ms. Wiggins.

Anna and Ms. Wiggins had noticed that as long as Acorn could see Winston, he followed their directions. But when he couldn't see Winston, Acorn would stop suddenly and refuse to go on.

"Acorn has a mind of his own," said Ms. Wiggins.

Anna knew that Acorn could be stubborn. But Anna could be stubborn, too. And

she was determined that Acorn would be a good driving pony. Anna signaled the turn again. "Walk on," Anna commanded. Acorn walked forward.

"Good for you, Anna," said Ms. Wiggins.

Anna drove Acorn around the ring three more times. Acorn continued to act stubborn, but so did Anna.

"You are both doing very well with your driving lessons," said Ms. Wiggins. "By next winter, you and Acorn can drive in the Winter Festival parade."

Winston, put his head over the fence and nickered.

Ms. Wiggins and Anna laughed.

"Winston wants Acorn to be in the parade, too," said Ms. Wiggins.

"Acorn and Winston are great friends," said Anna.

"That's because they're both Shetland ponies," said Ms. Wiggins.

"And because Winston is so wonderful," added Anna.

"This will be the twenty-fifth year Winston has led the Winter Festival parade," Ms. Wiggins said. "I think it's time for a younger pony to take over."

"Acorn and I don't want to be in the parade unless you and Winston are in it, too," said Anna.

"Then we'll just have two pony carts lead off the parade next year," said Ms. Wiggins.

Suddenly Acorn nickered and moved into a trot. "Whoa!" Anna ordered. She pulled on the lines. But Acorn trotted on.

Ms. Wiggins took the lines from Anna. "Halt," Ms. Wiggins ordered Acorn. Acorn obeyed Ms. Wiggins' command.

In the distance, Anna saw her friends, Pam and Lulu, riding their ponies toward them.

"He saw Lightning and Snow White," said Anna. "That's why he ran off like that."

"Acorn's going to need a lot of work," said Ms. Wiggins. "It's a good thing we didn't enter him in the parade *this* year."

Ms. Wiggins and Anna were unhitching

Acorn from the cart when Pam and Lulu rode up.

"How was your lesson?" Pam asked Anna.

"Okay," said Anna. "Driving is fun. But Acorn was acting stubborn."

"As usual," teased Lulu.

Pam and Lulu tied their ponies' lead ropes to rings on the paddock fence.

Ms. Wiggins led Winston over to the driving cart. "I'm taking Winston for a drive," she said. "Anna, why don't you help me hook him up? It'll be good practice for you."

Anna helped Ms. Wiggins while Pam and Lulu saddled up Acorn. After Ms. Wiggins put on Winston's bridle, she gave him a kiss on the cheek. "My sweet, old pony," she said.

"Shetland ponies live a long, long time, right?" Anna asked.

"Yes, they do. But Winston's already thirty years old," Ms. Wiggins said. She patted Winston on the shoulder and adjusted his bridle. Then she turned to the

Pony Pals. "I have a favor to ask you girls," she said.

"What?" they said together. The Pony Pals were happy if they could do a favor for Ms. Wiggins. She was always doing nice things for them. She let them ride on the trails of the Wiggins estate anytime they wanted.

"I'll be away for a week," said Ms. Wiggins. "I'm leaving for Boston tomorrow — for an art exhibit."

"Will your paintings be in the exhibit?" asked Anna.

Ms. Wiggins smiled. "Yes," she said. "Two of my big landscape paintings. Anyway, Mr. and Mrs. Silver will be taking care of things here while I'm gone. They'll do the chores for Winston and my horse, Picasso. But when you're trail riding around here, could you visit Picasso and Winston? They really enjoy being around you and your ponies."

"Sure," said Pam.

"We'll have a Pony Party with Winston and Picasso," added Anna.

The Pony Pals mounted their ponies for the trail ride home. And Ms. Wiggins climbed into the cart.

After they all said good-bye, the Pony Pals headed east toward the trails that led home. Ms. Wiggins directed Winston toward the hills to the west. Anna turned in her saddle and watched Ms. Wiggins's cart rolling along the trail.

Lulu called back to Anna, "You coming?"

Anna squeezed her legs to tell Acorn to walk on. They soon caught up to Lulu and Pam.

"I'm going to keep Acorn forever," Anna told her friends. "I'll drive him in a cart like Ms. Wiggins drives Winston. That way I'll never outgrow him. Ms. Wiggins said that by next year we'll be good enough to drive in the Winter Festival parade with her and Winston."

The Pony Pals pulled their ponies close together and raised their right hands. They hit high fives and cheered, "All right!"

Where's Winston?

The next morning Anna and Lulu did chores together for their ponies. Anna showed Lulu the bridle with blinkers, harness, and long lines that Ms. Wiggins had lent her. "I'm going to practice with Acorn at home all this week," Anna told Lulu.

"Can I help?" asked Lulu.

"Sure. You can help me ground drive around the paddock," said Anna. "If you walk in front of Acorn, it will be a big help."

"What's 'ground drive'?" asked Lulu.

"You walk behind your pony, holding on

to the long driving lines," said Anna. "You can do it, too."

"That'll be fun," said Lulu.

Anna and Lulu caught their ponies, brushed them, and saddled them up. They were meeting Pam and Lightning on Pony Pal Trail. The trail was a mile-and-a-half and cut through the woods separating Pam's house from Anna's and Lulu's. Pony Pal Trail also led to the many trails on Ms. Wiggins' estate.

Pam and Lightning were waiting for Anna and Lulu at the three birch trees in the middle of Pony Pal Trail. Anna halted Acorn next to Pam and Lightning. "I love winter vacation," Anna told Pam. "No school for a whole week!"

"Yeah," said Pam, "it's great."

Vacations were fun for all the Pony Pals — but Anna liked them best. Anna was dyslexic. So reading and math were difficult for her. What Anna loved was drawing, painting, horses, and vacation from school. Pam and Lulu liked school a lot better than Anna did.

Pam Crandal was a terrific student and an excellent reader. She loved horses, too. Her father was a veterinarian and her mother was a riding teacher. Pam couldn't remember a time when she didn't have a pony of her own.

"I can't wait until the Winter Festival on Saturday," said Pam. "You'll love it, Lulu. It's so much fun."

This was Lulu Sanders' first winter in Wiggins, so she had never been to the Winter Festival. Lulu's father studied wild animals and wrote about them. Lulu's mother died when she was little, so Lulu lived wherever her father was working. Recently Mr. Sanders decided that Lulu should live in one place for a while. So Lulu moved in with her grandmother.

Anna knew that Lulu missed her dad. But she loved that Lulu lived right next door to her and that their ponies shared a paddock.

The Pony Pals rode side by side across a large field. "Lulu, the Winter Festival has lots of neat things," said Pam. "First, there's the parade with bands, floats, and fire trucks from the towns around here."

"And my mother sets up a food tent," said Anna. "She sells hamburgers and hot dogs. She has hot drinks and brownies, too." Mrs. Harley owned the Off-Main Diner. Everyone in Wiggins loved her food, especially her famous brownies.

"There's a big crafts fair in Town Hall," Pam said.

"And a dance at night," added Anna. "Everybody goes. Even kids."

"It sounds great," said Lulu. "I can't wait."

When they reached the other end of the field, Anna said, "Let's go visit Winston and Picasso."

"Our ponies can rest and hang out with them," said Lulu.

"We can eat our lunches there," Pam added. "Let's go!"

Anna leaned over and patted Acorn on the neck. "We're going to see your old pal, Winston," she said.

The Pony Pals galloped the whole way to the Wiggins barn and paddocks before slowing to a walk. Picasso trotted over to the fence to greet them.

"Where's Winston?" Pam asked.

Acorn nickered as if to say, "Hey, Winston, I'm here. Where are you?" But Winston didn't trot over to them the way he usually did.

"Maybe the Silvers left him in the barn today," said Lulu.

"Why would they do that?" asked Anna. "They know Winston likes to be outside."

"Let's tie up our ponies and go look for him," said Pam.

Anna clipped on Acorn's lead rope and tied him to the fence. "I'll be right back to let you out in the paddock," she told him.

The girls climbed through the fence. When Anna was a few feet into the field, she noticed a pony on the ground in the far corner. She'd never seen Winston lying down, but she knew it must be him. She pointed and shouted, "There he is."

Anna ran across the field. Her heart beat faster and faster. Is Winston sick? she wondered. Is he injured?

Help!

Anna was running so fast her feet hardly touched the ground. Pam and Lulu were running toward Winston, too. But Anna was the first to reach the old gray pony.

Anna fell to her knees by Winston's side. He raised his head, looked up at her with sad eyes, and laid his head back down.

"Oh, Winston," Anna said. "What's wrong?"

Pam walked slowly around Winston. "It doesn't look like he broke any bones," she said. "But we can't be sure."

"Maybe he's sick with colic or something," said Lulu.

"We've got to do something," Anna said.

"This is a job for a veterinarian," said Pam. "I'll go to the house and call my dad."

"And I'll go to the barn and get a halter and lead rope," said Lulu. "If he gets up, we can take him to the barn."

"Look for the Silvers, too," said Anna. "Maybe they'll know what's wrong with Winston. I'll stay here."

While her friends were gone, Anna stroked Winston's neck and talked to him. She told him that he was a wonderful pony. Winston looked up at Anna. "Don't worry, Winston," she said. "We'll take care of you."

Winston rolled over so his feet were under him.

Lulu came back from the barn. "He wants to get up," Anna told her. "Give me the halter and lead rope."

Anna put the halter on Winston's head and attached the lead rope. "Come on, Winston," she said. She pulled on the rope.

"Stand up. You can do it." Winston struggled to stand. He was wobbly on his feet, but he was up.

Pam ran over to the two girls and the pony. "Winston, you're standing!" she said. "That's a good sign."

"Did you reach your dad?" asked Lulu.

Pam nodded. "He's on his way."

"I couldn't find the Silvers," Lulu said.

"Me either," said Pam. "They must have gone shopping or something."

"Let's see if Winston will walk to the barn," said Pam. "It's the best place for my dad to take care of him."

Anna stood in front of Winston. "Come on, Winston," she said. Winston took a step forward. And then another. And another.

Suddenly Winston stopped in his tracks. Anna was afraid he was going to lie down again. She pulled at the lead rope. "Come on, Winston," she said. "You're almost there."

Lulu gave Winston a little push.

"You can do it," said Pam.

Acorn saw Winston. He whinnied loudly. Winston looked in Acorn's direction, gave a low nicker, and walked on. Anna knew he was doing it for Acorn.

When Anna finally led Winston into his stall, he lay down with a thud.

"It was hard for him to walk," said Lulu.

"He was fine yesterday," said Anna. "What could be wrong?"

"It's my job to figure that out," said a man's voice.

"Dad!" said Pam. "You're here."

"Hi, girls," said Dr. Crandal.

Dr. Crandal squatted near Winston. "Well, old pony," he said. "Let's take a look at you."

The girls leaned over the stall door and watched Dr. Crandal examine Winston. First, he listened to Winston's heartbeat with a big stethoscope. Then he felt all the bones in his legs. Dr. Crandal talked to the pony as he checked inside his ears, nostrils, and mouth.

While Dr. Crandal was examining Winston, Mr. and Mrs. Silver came into the barn. "Goodness, goodness," Mr. Silver exclaimed. "What's going on?"

The girls told the Silvers everything that had happened. Mr. Silver leaned over the stall door and looked down at Winston. "Oh, my," he said. "I remember this pony when Ms. Wiggins first got him. What a lively little fellow he was." Mrs. Silver smiled at Anna. "Just like your Acorn."

"Ah, poor old pony," said Mr. Silver. "Has his time come, Doc?"

"I think so," said Dr. Crandal. "There's not much I can do for him."

Anna went over to Dr. Crandal and looked up at him. "Aren't you going to give him medicine and make him better?" she asked.

"We'll give him something for the congestion in his lungs," said Dr. Crandal. "But the best thing we can do for Winston is make sure he's comfortable and doesn't suffer. I wish I could talk to Ms. Wiggins."

"I have a phone number for her in Boston.

She's staying with friends," said Mr. Silver. "I'll go up to the house and write it out for you."

"What else can we do for him?" asked Anna.

"You can keep him warm," said Dr. Crandal. "And make him a warm mash. But don't worry if he doesn't eat it."

"He has to eat if he's going to get better," said Anna. "And shouldn't he stand up?" she asked.

"Let him rest for now," said Dr. Crandal. "But if he stands up later that'd be good. It's a bad sign when an old pony won't get up."

"I want to stay with him tonight," said Anna. "Ms. Wiggins would want me to."

"We could all stay here," said Lulu. "And have turns taking care of Winston."

"Can we, Dad?" asked Pam.

Dr. Crandal thought about it for a few seconds. "What do you two think?" he asked Mr. and Mrs. Silver. "Could you put up with these gals tonight?"

"If Ms. Wiggins were here she'd be up all night with Winston herself," said Mr. Silver. "She loves that pony."

"And we have plenty of beds," added Mrs. Silver.

"Could we sleep in the barn?" asked Pam. "That's what we usually do for sleepovers."

"The tack room is heated," said Mr. Silver. "I suppose you could."

Anna knew that if Pam had permission to stay over, she'd get permission, too.

"My grandmother will let me stay if you both can," said Lulu.

Acorn whinnied loudly. He seemed to be saying, "What's going on in there? Where's my pal, Winston?"

Anna had an idea. "Dr. Crandal, can Acorn stay in the stall next to Winston tonight?" she asked. "They're very good friends."

"I don't see why not," said Dr. Crandal.

Before Dr. Crandal left, he told the girls and the Silvers to telephone him if Winston's condition changed.

Anna went out to the barn to get Acorn. She gave him a hug. "Winston is very sick," she said. Acorn nickered and nuzzled into Anna's shoulder. "Don't worry, Acorn," she said. "We'll make Winston better. The Pony Pals have solved tough problems before. And we'll solve this one."

Night Watch

The Pony Pals took care of Winston all day. At dinnertime, Mr. Silver came into the barn. "You girls go up to the house and eat your supper," he said. "I'll stay with Winston."

Mrs. Silver had made them spaghetti, salad, and apple pie. When they finished eating, Pam and Lulu stayed to help with the dishes. Anna went back to the barn to take Mr. Silver's place. She was disappointed to see Winston still lying down.

"Did he eat anything?" Anna asked.

Mr. Silver shook his head. "He's just been lying there," he said. "Doc Crandal stopped to check on him and drop off your sleeping bags. I put them in the tack room."

"What did he say about Winston?"

"Just to call him if there's a change, Anna," said Mr. Silver. He shook his head sadly. "It doesn't seem like Winston's ever going to get up again."

When Lulu and Pam came back to the barn, the Pony Pals made out a chart with a schedule for their night's watch.

	Food	Water	Standing
8-10 Pam			
10-12 Lulu			
12-2 Anna			
2-4 Pam			
4-6 Mr. Silver			
6-8 Lulu			
8-10 Anna			

Wake others and phone Dr. C. if Winston seems to be suffering.

At eight o'clock, Pam began her watch. Anna and Lulu went to the tack room. They laid out their sleeping bags and slipped into them. They fell asleep talking about Winston.

"Anna, wake up." Anna opened her eyes. Lulu was leaning over her. "It's your turn," she said.

Anna unzipped her sleeping bag. She still had on her clothes. She put on her boots and splashed cold water on her face. Lulu handed her a container of apple juice and a box of cookies.

"Did Winston stand up?" Anna asked Lulu.

"He's been sleeping lying down," said Lulu. "He slept the whole time." Lulu was already snuggled up in her sleeping bag. "Good night," she said.

Anna left the tack room and went to the horse stalls. Acorn was sleeping on his feet — as usual. Anna looked at Winston lying in the straw. She remembered what Mr. Silver said: "It doesn't look like the old pony will ever get up again."

▄▄▄▄▄▄▄▄▄▄▄▄ went into the stall and sat next to Winston. She felt like crying. Poor Winston! He acted so sick. How come no one was trying to save his life? How could they just let him die?

Anna thought Ms. Wiggins wouldn't give up on Winston. Everything would be different if Ms. Wiggins were here. Ms. Wiggins had trusted the Pony Pals to watch out for Winston. Anna had to do something.

Acorn woke up and nickered softly. He could see Anna through the bars that separated the stalls. "Acorn," Anna said, "we're not going to let Winston die." She scratched Winston's head through the thick mane. "Wake up, Winston," she said. "Time to stand up."

First Anna tried bribing Winston with a carrot. He wasn't interested. Next, she tried pushing him. No luck. She put on his halter and lead rope and tried pulling him upright. But Winston didn't budge. He looked up at Anna and gave a weak whinny as if to say, "Leave me alone."

But Anna didn't give up. "Get up, Winston," she said. "You have to." Winston suddenly rolled onto his legs and slowly stood up. "You did it, Winston!" Anna said excitedly.

Acorn nickered at Winston. The old pony looked back at Acorn. But he was too sick and too tired to make any sound.

"Now it's time to eat," said Anna. She held the mash out to Winston. But he didn't want it. "Do you want water first?" asked Anna. He didn't want water, either. "Well at least you're standing," Anna told him.

At two o'clock Anna was supposed to wake up Pam. But she didn't want to leave Winston alone, even for a minute. She was afraid he'd lie down again.

Around two-thirty, Pam came to take her turn. "Why didn't you wake me up?" she asked Anna.

"Look," Anna said. She pointed to Winston.

"He's standing!" said Pam.

"If he's standing he can get better," said Anna. "I know he can. Try to get him to drink and eat during your watch. And don't let him lie down. He can sleep standing up, just the way he always did."

"It's great that he's standing," said Pam. She stroked the old pony's cheek. "Good for you, Winston."

Anna went back to the tack room to sleep. She needed her rest. Tomorrow she was going to be taking care of Winston. Tomorrow she was going to make Winston better. She crawled into her sleeping bag and fell asleep.

Anna woke up suddenly. Where was she? She looked around and saw that she was in Ms. Wiggins' barn. And she remembered that Winston was sick. She unzipped her sleeping bag and pulled on her boots. Pam's and Lulu's sleeping bags were empty. Anna glanced at her watch. Eight-thirty. She'd overslept.

Anna ran out of the tack room toward Winston's stall. Lulu and Pam were standing in the aisle of the barn talking.

Lulu saw Anna first. "Hi, sleepyhead," she said. "We cleaned Acorn's stall and fed him for you."

"Where's Winston?" asked Anna. Before they could answer, Anna saw where Winston was. He was lying on the floor of his stall. "How come he's lying down?" she said. "What happened?"

"He went down about halfway through my turn," said Pam.

"You were supposed to keep him on his feet," said Anna. She was angry. "It was important," she shouted.

Acorn nickered as if to say, "What's wrong?" Winston opened his eyes, looked at Anna, and shut them again.

Mr. Silver came into the barn. "Breakfast is ready, girls," he said. "I'll stay with Winston."

"I'm not hungry," said Anna. "I'll stay here." She turned her back on Pam and Lulu.

Lulu put a hand on Anna's shoulder. "It's not Pam's fault that Winston went back down," said Lulu.

"There's nothing more we can do for Winston," said Pam.

Anna glared at Pam and Lulu. What was *wrong* with her friends? The Pony Pals never gave up on a problem. "I'm not giving up," she said.

The Phone Call

Pam and Lulu went up to the house for breakfast. But Anna stayed with Winston. She put his halter and lead rope back on him. "Come on, Winston," she said. "It's time to stand up. You can do it." She gave a little pull on the lead rope. Winston didn't budge.

"Let him be, Anna," a man's voice said. Anna looked up. It was Dr. Crandal.

"He stood up last night," Anna said. "For about two hours."

Dr. Crandal looked at the chart the girls

had made. "I see," he said. "But he didn't have any food or water. Let's take a look at you, Winston."

Anna left the stall while Dr. Crandal examined Winston. Anna leaned over the gate and watched. "What's wrong with him?" she asked. "What disease does he have?"

"Winston doesn't have a disease," said Dr. Crandal. "He's dying of old age. All his systems are giving out. His heart, his lungs, his digestive system."

"Can't you fix them?" Anna said.

Dr. Crandal shook his head. "Sometimes you just have to let nature take its course, Anna," he said.

Mr. Silver came into the barn and stood beside Anna. "What do you think, Doc?" he asked.

"Same thing as I thought last night," said Dr. Crandal. "Winston is dying. I'd like to put him out with an injection tonight."

"Ms. Wiggins wouldn't want him to suffer," said Mr. Silver. "That's a fact."

"I haven't been able to reach her," Dr. Crandal said. "I want to talk to her before I put him down."

"She knew Winston might not make it through the winter," said Mr. Silver. "I dug a hole before the ground froze, just in case."

Dr. Crandal and Mr. Silver were talking about putting Winston to sleep forever. Anna didn't know what to say or do. *Everyone* was giving up on Winston.

Pam and Lulu came into the barn. "Anna, Mrs. Silver said to go up to the house for pancakes," said Pam.

"She makes great blueberry pancakes," said Lulu.

"I'm not hungry," said Anna. How could Pam and Lulu think of food now?

Pam went into the stall and stood by her father. "Morning, honey," he said.

"Hi, Dad. How's Winston?" Pam asked.

"It's time to say good-bye to Winston," Dr. Crandal answered.

"We'll stay with him, Dad," said Pam quietly.

"I'll stop by between my other barn calls," Dr. Crandal said.

"Isn't there something we can do to make him better?" asked Lulu.

"He won't get better," said Dr. Crandal. "Just keep him comfortable."

"What if he stands up again?" asked Anna.

"I don't think he will," said Dr. Crandal. "He hasn't the strength." Dr. Crandal went up to the house to telephone Ms. Wiggins in Boston.

The Pony Pals were alone with Winston. "Poor old pony," said Pam. "We'll miss you." Pam was crying.

"Ms. Wiggins is going to feel so bad she wasn't here," said Lulu. She was crying too.

Anna wasn't crying. She was too angry to cry. "Why are you giving up on Winston?" she asked. "We're the Pony Pals. We're supposed to solve problems."

"I saw a horse die of old age once," said Pam. "He acted just like Winston."

"And Dr. Crandal said there's no hope," said Lulu. "He should know."

Anna thought, Dr. Crandal is the problem. We need to find another veterinarian. One who would try to save Winston's life instead of killing him. Dr. Crandal was Pam's father. So Anna didn't tell Pam her idea. She needed to talk to Ms. Wiggins. "I'm going up to the house," she told Pam and Lulu.

"We'll stay here with Winston," said Pam.

Anna ran all the way to the house. Dr. Crandal was talking on the phone. "Okay," he said into the phone. "I'll call you when it's over." Anna knew he was talking to Ms. Wiggins.

"I want to talk to Ms. Wiggins, too," Anna told Dr. Crandal.

"Hold on," Dr. Crandal said into the phone. "Anna Harley wants to talk to you. This is pretty rough on the girls."

Anna took the phone. She was glad that Dr. Crandal left right away.

"Hi," she said to Ms. Wiggins.

"Hello, Anna," Ms. Wiggins said back. "I

hear my poor old Winston is dying." Anna could tell Ms. Wiggins was crying.

"Winston can't die," said Anna.

"Dr. Crandal says he's dying," said Ms. Wiggins.

"Winston stood up for me last night," Anna said. "Dr. Crandal doesn't even try to make him stand up. He's given up on Winston. I think we should get another doctor."

"Anna, I trust Dr. Crandal," said Ms. Wiggins.

"Please," said Anna. "My mother will help me find another doctor. I know Winston can get better. I just know it."

"Anna, I'm sorry that I'm not there," Ms. Wiggins said. "Maybe then I could help you understand. Winston's had a long, wonderful life. I want him to die peacefully. It's time to say good-bye to Winston. Will you say good-bye for me?"

"Aren't you coming home?" asked Anna.

"I might not make it in time," said Ms. Wiggins.

Anna was shocked. Ms. Wiggins wouldn't let her get another veterinarian. And she wasn't even going to be there to say good-bye to Winston herself.

As Anna was hanging up the phone, Pam came running into the hall. "Winston is standing up!" she shouted. "Hurry, Anna."

Anna ran back to the barn with Pam. She thought, maybe *I'm* right and everyone else is wrong. Maybe we can still save Winston's life.

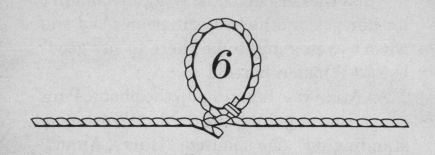

Bad Pony!

Anna and Pam ran into the barn. Pam pointed toward the stalls. "Look," she said.

Anna saw that Winston was standing. His head reached over the stall door. Acorn's head was hanging over his door, too. Winston and Acorn were looking at one another and rubbing noses. Lulu stood nearby. She smiled at Anna. Pam and Anna walked quietly toward Lulu and the ponies.

"How did you get Winston to stand up?" asked Anna.

"We didn't do it," said Lulu. "Acorn did."

"He nickered at Winston until he got up," Pam said.

"Acorn," Anna said, "you're a great nurse and friend."

Acorn didn't look at Anna. All of his attention was on Winston.

"I'm going to put Winston's lead rope back on," said Anna. "So we can keep him standing. Lulu, will you make him a fresh warm mash? Maybe he'll finally eat something."

Suddenly, Anna saw Acorn give Winston a little push with his nozzle.

"Acorn, don't!" said Anna. "Don't push him!"

But it was too late. Winston took a wobbly step backward and lay down in a heap on the straw.

"You're a bad pony, Acorn," Anna scolded. "Why did you do that?"

Acorn ignored Anna. He turned in his stall and looked down at Winston through the bars.

"Don't scold Acorn," Pam told Anna. "He didn't do anything wrong."

Anna opened the door to Acorn's stall and went in. "He pushed Winston over," she said angrily.

"I think he was just telling Winston that it is okay to die," said Lulu.

"And saying good-bye," added Pam.

Anna didn't care what her friends thought. She slipped on Acorn's halter. "I'm putting Acorn in the paddock," she said. "Then I'll get Winston to stand up."

"Anna, let Winston die in peace," said Pam.

"He's not dying," shouted Anna. She pulled on Acorn's lead rope. "Come on, Acorn," she said. "I'm putting you outside."

Acorn pulled against Anna. He didn't want to leave the stall.

"Anna," said Pam, "Acorn doesn't want to go outside. He wants to stay here with Winston."

Winston took a deep, noisy breath and closed his eyes.

"Don't you want to say good-bye to Winston, too?" asked Lulu.

Anna looked at Winston through the bars of Acorn's stall. He lay in a heap. Anna tried to imagine him standing up. Or eating hay. Or running around the paddock. Or pulling the driving cart. But she couldn't picture Winston doing any of the things he used to do. And she finally understood that Acorn, Lulu, and Pam were right. Winston was dying.

Anna took off Acorn's halter. She put her face against his cheek. "I'm sorry I yelled at you," she said. Then she went into Winston's stall.

Lulu was gently brushing his mane with her fingers. "Good-bye Winston," she said.

Pam stroked Winston's neck. "You're a wonderful pony, Winston. Ms. Wiggins loves you very much," she told him.

Anna sat beside her friends. She felt tears coming down her cheek. "I don't want him to die," she whispered.

"I know," said Lulu. "Me either."

"I think it's almost the end," said Pam.

"I'll go find Mr. Silver," said Lulu softly. She stood up and left the stall.

Anna leaned over and whispered into Winston's ear, "Ms. Wiggins says good-bye. Good-bye, wonderful Winston. I'll miss you."

A choking sound came from Winston's throat.

Anna remembered that Ms. Wiggins said she wanted Winston to have a peaceful end. And she remembered what Dr. Crandal said about giving Winston an injection to help him die. "Call your father, Pam," said Anna. "We don't want Winston to suffer."

"Okay," said Pam.

Winston's whole body started shaking. Anna had never seen an animal shiver like that. She felt frightened for the old pony. Suddenly, the shivering stopped and Winston's body went limp.

Acorn whinnied a low, sad sound.

Mr. Silver and Lulu rushed into the stall. Mr. Silver squatted beside Winston. He put his head on Winston's barrel-side and listened. Then he put his hand in front of Winston's nose to feel if there was any breath going in and out. Finally, he said, "It was a peaceful end, wasn't it?"

"Yes," said Anna, "very peaceful."

"Just the way Ms. Wiggins wanted it to be," Mr. Silver said.

"I'll call my father," said Pam.

"And tell Mrs. Silver, please." Mr. Silver said. "She was very fond of this pony. We all were." Anna saw tears in Mr. Silver's eyes.

"I'll go with you," Lulu told Pam.

"You coming, Anna?" Pam asked. Anna shook her head.

Pam and Lulu left the barn.

Anna touched Winston's mane one last time. Then she helped Mr. Silver cover Winston's body with a blanket.

Anna went into Acorn's stall. She put her arms around her own pony's neck and cried.

Too Late

Anna put on Acorn's halter and lead rope. He followed her out of the stall.

Anna led her pony to the paddock. "Acorn, you've been inside for a day and night," said Anna. "That's the most you've been indoors since I got you." When Anna let Acorn free, he threw back his head and galloped across the field.

Lightning and Snow White were grazing in the field. They whinnied hellos to Acorn and joined him in his run.

Anna noticed a car coming up the long

driveway. It went past the house and drove up to the barn. Ms. Wiggins stepped out of the car. Anna called out her name and ran to her.

"I came as fast as I could," Ms. Wiggins said. "Anna, am I too late?"

Anna nodded. "Winston died a little while ago." She pointed to the barn. "He's still in there," she said.

Ms. Wiggins turned and walked into the barn. Anna wondered if she should go with her. Then she thought, If it was Acorn who died, I'd want to be alone with him. Anna decided to stay outside and wait for Ms. Wiggins.

Anna noticed Mrs. Silver, Lulu, and Pam come out the back door of the house. They were walking toward the barn. Anna met them near the paddock.

"Ms. Wiggins is back," Anna said. "She's in the barn."

"We saw the car," Pam said.

"She arrived just a few minutes too late," said Mrs. Silver sadly.

"I'd feel so awful if something happened to my pony and I wasn't there," said Lulu.

"Me, too," said Pam.

Mrs. Silver and the Pony Pals waited for Ms. Wiggins by the barn door. No one talked.

Finally, Ms. Wiggins came out. Her eyes were red from crying. In one hand she had the chart that the Pony Pals made for taking care of Winston. In the other hand she carried a thick braid of Winston's mane.

"Thank you for staying with him, girls," she said. She held up the chart. "What you did for Winston and me was so wonderful. I'll never forget it."

"We wanted to help," said Pam.

"Acorn helped, too," said Anna. "He stayed in the stall next to Winston the whole time."

Ms. Wiggins looked at the three ponies and Picasso in the paddock. "Acorn's a terrific pony," she said.

"He's going to miss Winston," said Anna.

"We all will," said Lulu.

Tears were streaming down Ms. Wiggins'

cheeks. The Pony Pals were crying, too. Mrs. Silver put her arm around Ms. Wiggins' shoulder. "Come have some tea, dear," she said. "And maybe a little something to eat."

Ms. Wiggins looked around at the Pony Pals. "Will you come, too?" she asked. "Please."

They nodded that they would.

"Anna didn't have breakfast yet," said Lulu.

Ms. Wiggins smiled at Anna. "Neither did I. Maybe we can convince Mrs. Silver to make us blueberry pancakes."

"The batter is already made," said Mrs. Silver.

Mrs. Silver made pancakes for everyone. And even though Anna felt sad, she was glad to be eating. While they ate, Ms. Wiggins told them stories about Winston. Anna particularly liked the stories from when Ms. Wiggins was her age.

"Once, when I was out alone with him," she said, "I got off to look at a beaver dam.

I accidentally stepped in a hole and twisted my ankle very badly. I couldn't walk. And I couldn't mount Winston again. It was winter and very cold. I was quite frightened. I found a long stick lying near me. I used it to tap Winston and told him to go home. He trotted off. My parents found him on the front lawn. When they saw he was saddled up and alone, they knew something bad had happened. Winston led them to me."

"Winston was a hero," said Pam.

"And a best friend," said Ms. Wiggins.

After breakfast, Ms. Wiggins took out a photo album with pictures of her and Winston. In some pictures Ms. Wiggins was a kid riding Winston. In others, she was a grown-up driving him in a cart. Several of the photos were from the Wiggins Winter Festival parade. Ms. Wiggins and Winston looked happy and proud in those pictures.

Ms. Wiggins closed the photo album. Anna knew that she was feeling tired and sad. "We'd better go," Anna said.

"Thank you for staying with me," Ms. Wiggins said. "And for taking care of Winston."

The Pony Pals didn't talk while they saddled up their ponies. And they were quiet as they rode the Wiggins trails toward Pony Pal Trail. They halted their ponies at the three birches.

"I feel awful for Ms. Wiggins," said Anna.

"I wish we could do something for her," said Lulu.

"We're on vacation, so we have plenty of time to do something really special," said Pam.

"Let's each come up with an idea," said Lulu.

The Pony Pals agreed to meet at Off-Main Diner the next morning to share their ideas.

Anna and Lulu turned their ponies toward home. Anna galloped along Pony Pal Trail. What could the Pony Pals do that would make Ms. Wiggins feel better?

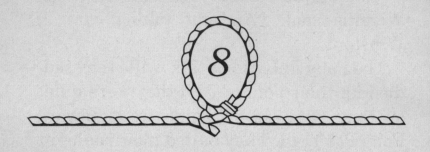

At the Diner

The next morning Anna and Lulu walked over to Off-Main Diner. They saw Lightning tied to the hitching post out front. Lulu and Anna gave Lightning some hello pats and went inside. Pam was already sitting in the Pony Pals' favorite booth. A folded piece of notepaper was on the table in front of her. "Let's share our ideas before we eat anything," said Pam.

Anna was holding a rolled-up piece of drawing paper. Lulu took a small notebook from her jacket pocket.

"You go first, Lulu," said Pam.
Lulu read:

Make a donation to Saint Francis
Animal Shelter in memory of Winston.

"That's a great idea," said Pam.

"But I don't have any money," said Anna. "I spent all my allowance on supplies for Acorn."

"I thought maybe we could collect money from people at the Winter Festival," said Lulu.

"Everyone in town knows Winston from all the years he was in the parade," said Pam. "They'll want to give money."

"I'll decorate a shoe box with drawings of Winston," said Anna. "People can put their donations in that."

"Good idea, Anna," said Lulu.

"What's your idea, Pam?" asked Anna.

Pam read her idea out loud.

Make a sign for Winston.

"We could carry it in the parade," Pam explained.

"I love that idea," said Lulu.

"My idea is about the parade, too," said Anna.

She unrolled her drawing paper and laid it out in the middle of the table.

"My idea is that Ms. Wiggins can drive Acorn in the parade," Anna said. "She wanted Acorn to take Winston's place. I think it would make her feel better if Acorn could do it this year."

"Acorn's only pulled a cart a few times," said Pam. "And the parade is the day after tomorrow."

"Acorn's really smart," said Lulu. "I bet he could do it." She smiled at Anna. "And you learned a lot about driving from Ms. Wiggins. You can train Acorn. We'll help you."

"I don't know," said Pam. "Teaching a pony to drive is a big job."

"We could put the sign about Winston on the back of the driving cart," said Lulu.

"We don't even *have* a driving cart," said Pam.

"But Ms. Wiggins lent me the equipment for ground driving," said Anna. "Let's work with Acorn first. Then we can figure out how to get a cart."

"We have to begin somewhere," said Lulu. "Let's go."

"I guess it's worth a try," said Pam.

Anna went behind the counter and packed up apple juice and doughnuts to go. Her mother came out from the kitchen with a bunch of carrots for the ponies. The Pony Pals didn't tell Mrs. Harley that they were going to train Acorn for the parade. They wanted to surprise everyone.

As soon as they were back at the Harley paddock, the girls started working with Acorn. Anna put on the harness and bridle with blinders. Then she stood behind him holding the long lines. Lulu and Pam stood nearby to help.

"Walk on," Anna called to Acorn. He stood still. His ears went back. Anna told him to walk on again. This time she flicked the lash of the whip against his side. Acorn still didn't move.

"Maybe he's forgotten everything he learned," said Pam.

"Maybe he's being stubborn," said Anna. "Pam, go to his head and give him a pull."

Pam pulled on the lead rope and Acorn walked forward. But when Anna told him to halt he backed up.

Lulu and Pam came over to Anna. "He doesn't obey you when you're ground driving him," Pam said. "It's not safe to hitch him to a cart. Even if we had one."

"There has to be a way we can train Acorn in time to be in the parade," said Lulu. "We can't give up."

"Then we need help," said Pam. "We need a good driving teacher."

"What about your mother, Pam?" asked Anna. "She knows how to drive."

"My mom's going to a special workshop for riding teachers this week," said Pam. "Besides, our driving cart is broken."

"Maybe we should ask Ms. Wiggins to teach Acorn," said Lulu.

"She's too sad to do it," said Anna.

"Besides, we want to surprise her," said Pam.

"Who else could help us?" asked Anna.

"It has to be someone who's an excellent driving teacher," said Lulu.

"And has the equipment," said Pam.

"And who will do it for free," added Anna.

Anna thought hard. Who did they know who could teach Acorn?

A Challenge for Acorn

Lulu and Pam watched Anna take the driving equipment off Acorn. They were all thinking about who could train Acorn in carriage driving.

"I've got it!" shouted Anna. "Mr. Olson!"

"He knows a lot about horses and driving," said Pam.

"And Mr. Olson is a good friend of Ms. Wiggins, too," said Lulu. "I'll bet he'd do it for her."

"Let's go ask him," said Anna.

The girls tacked up their ponies. They

rode east on Main Street to Belgo Road. They took Belgo Road past the diner. Then they made a left onto a dirt trail that went through the woods.

The trail that led to Mr. Olson's farm was one of Anna's favorite rides. But that day she didn't enjoy it. She was worried that Mr. Olson wouldn't be on his horse farm. Or that he wouldn't have time to train Acorn. Or that he'd say Acorn couldn't learn in time for the parade.

"There's Mr. Olson!" shouted Lulu. She pointed to the riding ring. The Pony Pals rode up to Mr. Olson.

"Hello there," called Mr. Olson. He came out of the ring to meet them.

"Ms. Wiggins' pony died," said Anna.

"I heard," he said. "Poor Ms. Wiggins. She loved that pony. Winston was the best driving pony around these parts." Anna thought she saw tears in Mr. Olson's eyes. "We'll miss him in the parade this year."

"That's what we came to talk to you about," said Pam.

"Ms. Wiggins was teaching Anna and Acorn driving," said Lulu, "so Acorn could take Winston's place in the parade someday."

"We want to surprise her by putting Acorn in the parade *this* year," said Anna.

"But Acorn's not that good, yet," said Pam. "Will you give him some lessons?"

Mr. Olson rubbed Acorn's muzzle. "How many times has he been hitched up to the cart?" he asked Anna.

"Just a few," said Anna. "But he was pretty good at it."

"And you think he'd be ready to lead a parade in two days?" Mr. Olson asked.

"Acorn's a smart pony," she said.

Mr. Olson didn't say anything for a minute. He looked Acorn in the eye and thought for a minute. Finally he said, "Get that saddle off him, Anna, and let's see what he can do." He looked over at Lulu and Pam. "You two are going to have to help," he said. "And it's not going to be all fun."

"We know," said Lulu as she slid off Snow White.

"We're doing it for Ms. Wiggins," said Pam. She dismounted Lightning.

Mr. Olson pointed to a paddock near the barn. "Put Lightning and Snow White in there," he said. "Then meet me in the barn. You can help bring out the cart and harness. Anna, unsaddle Acorn and wait for me in the ring. We'll start our work there."

First, Mr. Olson ground drove Acorn. Acorn was better behaved for him than he was for Anna. But he still stopped sometimes without being told. "He knows what to do," said Mr. Olson. "He's just being stubborn."

"I know," said Anna.

Mr. Olson hitched Acorn to the cart. He and Anna climbed into the seat. Lulu and Pam stood near Acorn's head and encouraged him to behave. But Acorn wasn't behaving very well.

The three girls and Mr. Olson worked

with Acorn all afternoon. It was a windy winter's day. Anna had on gloves and thick socks, but her hands and feet were still cold. And she knew Pam and Lulu were cold and tired from running around the ring next to Acorn. Once, Lulu slipped in the icy mud. Everyone was working hard and no one complained.

At three o'clock Mr. Olson said, "Enough for today." He shook his head. Anna knew he was discouraged about Acorn. "He could be a terrific little driving pony," Mr. Olson said. "But I doubt we can have him ready for the parade."

"Can we try?" asked Anna. "Please."

"For Ms. Wiggins' sake," added Lulu.

"I'll leave it up to you girls," Mr. Olson said. "If you come by tomorrow, I'll do my part. But I'm warning you, it doesn't look like he'll be good enough for the parade this year."

The Pony Pals rode slowly along the trail. They were cold and tired.

"Let's stop at the diner for some hot chocolate," Anna suggested.

"And talk about what to do," added Lulu. They tied their ponies to the hitching post in front of the diner and went in. Mrs. Harley made the Pony Pals hot chocolate and grilled cheese sandwiches. They took them in the back to their favorite booth.

The Pony Pals ate and drank silently for a while. Then Pam said, "I don't think Acorn will be ready in time for the parade. Mr. Olson doesn't either."

"Vacation is almost over," said Lulu. "We haven't done half the things we planned."

"Like exploring over near Mt. Morris," said Pam.

Anna listened to her friends. Maybe they were right. Maybe Acorn couldn't learn to be a good driving pony so fast. Maybe she was asking too much of her friends. Maybe she was asking too much of Acorn.

Balloons and Music

"Hello, girls."

Anna looked up.

Ms. Wiggins was walking toward the booth. "I saw three very cute ponies in front of the diner," she said. "So I came in to say hello."

Ms. Wiggins didn't look as tired as she did the day before. But she still looked sad. "Thank you again for everything you did for Winston and me," she said.

"You're welcome," the Pony Pals said.

Ms. Wiggins noticed the poster on the

wall near the booth. It was for the Winter Festival. "Winston just missed being in the parade," she said. "I wish I'd started teaching Acorn driving earlier. Now we'll have to wait until next year, Anna."

Mrs. Harley came over and gave Ms. Wiggins a hug. "Sorry about your pony," she said. "Come have a cup of coffee with me." The two women went to the counter.

When they were gone, the Pony Pals leaned forward to whisper to one another.

"She'd be so glad if Acorn was in the parade," said Lulu.

"We have to try," said Pam. "We'll work all day tomorrow. No matter how cold it is."

"We won't give up," said Anna.

Then Anna had a terrible thought. She told it to her friends. "What if Acorn is in the parade, but Ms. Wiggins isn't there to see him?"

"Look, Ms. Wiggins is leaving," said Lulu.

"We have to make sure she's coming to the parade," said Anna. "Let's go."

The girls rushed out of the diner. Ms. Wiggins was heading toward her car.

" 'Bye, Ms. Wiggins," Lulu said.

" 'Bye, girls," Ms. Wiggins said over her shoulder.

"See you at the parade," added Anna.

Ms. Wiggins stopped and turned to them. "I've decided not to go to the parade this year," she said.

The Pony Pals looked at one another. They had to think of something fast.

"But we're doing something special at the parade," said Pam. "It's in memory of Winston."

"It would be nice if you were there," added Lulu.

Anna was afraid Pam and Lulu were going to give away the surprise by telling Ms. Wiggins that they were training Acorn to be in the parade.

"What are you doing for Winston?" asked Ms. Wiggins.

Anna tried to signal Pam not to say their

plan. Pam winked at Anna and told Ms. Wiggins, "We're going to raise money in memory of Winston."

"And donate it to St. Francis Animal Shelter," added Lulu.

Anna smiled at her friends.

"It would be great if you were at the parade," Anna told Ms. Wiggins.

"What a sweet thing for you girls to do," said Ms. Wiggins. She looked at each of the girls. "A donation to the shelter is a wonderful way to remember Winston. I will see you at the parade."

Ms. Wiggins left and the Pony Pals went to their ponies at the hitching post. "So she wasn't coming to the parade," said Lulu.

"But now she is," said Pam.

"And we only told her one of our three surprises," said Anna. "That was so smart, Pam."

"It was the only thing I could think of," said Pam.

Anna patted Acorn on the neck. "Now all

we have to do is turn Acorn into a terrific driving pony," she said.

The next morning the Pony Pals were at Mr. Olson's farm by nine o'clock. It was a sunny winter day. Everyone was rested and ready for a day of hard work.

The first few times around the ring, Acorn acted as stubborn as the day before. But Mr. Olson knew how to make Acorn pay attention to him. Anna loved riding in the cart, especially when Mr. Olson turned the lines and whip over to her.

"Now we'll go on the driving trail that cuts through the fields," Mr. Olson said. Pam opened the gate. When Acorn was out of the fenced-in ring, he broke into a trot. Mr. Olson scolded and pulled hard on the lines. Acorn halted. Mr. Olson shook his head. Anna knew he was wondering if Acorn could possibly be ready for the parade. But Mr. Olson didn't give up. He kept on working with Acorn and Anna.

After lunch, Mr. Olson handed Lulu a bunch of balloons and a pile of sticks. "You girls blow up these balloons and tie them to the sticks," he said. He pulled two noise-makers out of his jacket pocket. "You'll need these, too."

"Are we having a party?" Anna asked.

"Sort of," said Mr. Olson. "Pam and Lulu are going to wave the balloons, shout, and use the noisemakers near Acorn while he's pulling the cart. He has to be used to the noises of the parade."

"What about music?" asked Anna. "There'll be bands at the parade."

"Good thinking," Mr. Olson said. "There's a radio in the tack room."

The next time Mr. Olson and Anna drove Acorn over the trails, Pam and Lulu ran beside the pony waving the balloons and making noise. Loud music blared from the radio.

Acorn was a little confused at first. He couldn't see where the noise was coming

from because of the blinders. By the third time over the trails, Acorn was used to the noise.

When the lesson was over, they were all tired. Pam and Lulu were hoarse from shouting.

"Is Acorn good enough to be in the parade?" Anna asked Mr. Olson.

"I'm not sure," Mr. Olson said. "I won't know until tomorrow morning. I'll bring the cart to your place early. We can try driving Acorn on the parade route while they're setting up. It'll be a test. If we can drive him on Main Street without any problems, he can be in the parade."

Anna knew that Acorn wasn't a terrific driving pony yet. But Mr. Olson was giving him a chance. Was there anything the Pony Pals could do to help Acorn pass Mr. Olson's driving test?

The Winter Festival

The next morning, the Pony Pals met in Anna's kitchen. She showed them the box she had made for contributions in memory of Winston.

"We'll pass around the donation box, Anna," said Lulu "You'll be busy driving Acorn with Mr. Olson."

"I don't know if Acorn can do it," Anna said. "He wasn't very good yesterday."

"Mr. Olson said if he isn't perfect this morning, he can't be in the parade," said Pam.

"Why isn't he being a good driving pony?" asked Lulu. "Ms. Wiggins said he'd be good."

"I think he misses Winston," said Lulu.

"I wish Winston was here to drive in front of him," said Pam. "Then I bet Acorn would be fine."

"Acorn loves to be with his pony friends," said Lulu.

Anna had an idea. "That's it!" she shouted. "I know what we can do so Acorn will drive better." She jumped up. "Hurry. Let's go to the paddock. We have to be ready when Mr. Olson gets here."

"Ready for what?" asked Pam.

As they ran to the paddock, Anna told them her plan.

When Mr. Olson's pickup pulled into the driveway with the cart, the Pony Pals were ready. "Bring Acorn here," he told Anna. "Well hook him up to the cart in the driveway."

Anna led Acorn out of the paddock and up the driveway. Pam and Lulu followed, riding Lightning and Snow White. Mr. Olson was surprised to see them on their ponies. "I thought you two were going to help us with the driving," he said.

"We are helping," said Lulu.

"We're going to ride in front of Acorn," said Pam.

"If Acorn's friends are walking in front of him, he'll work better," said Anna. "I just know it."

Mr. Olson smiled. "The Pony Pals are always coming up with powerful ideas," he said. "It's worth a try."

Main Street was closed to traffic. People were preparing for the Winter Festival. A tent and booths were being put up on the Town Green. Mr. Harley was starting a fire in the volunteer firemen's huge barbecue pit. And the band was warming up.

Anna knew that the activity wouldn't bother Snow White and Lightning. And it wouldn't bother Acorn, if she were riding him. But today Acorn was pulling a cart and wearing blinders.

Anna and Mr. Olson climbed into the cart.

Pam and Lulu took the lead down Main Street. Anna held her breath. Mr. Olson signaled Acorn to follow. Acorn walked behind his pony friends and kept a good pace. Suddenly a policeman ran into the road. He blew a whistle and signaled the Pony Pal parade to stop. A group of Boy Scouts, shouting and laughing, ran across the road in front of them. Snow White and Lightning stood quietly. So did Acorn.

Mr. Olson turned to Anna and smiled. "I have a feeling Acorn will pass this test," he said.

Half an hour later, the Pony Pals were in the school parking lot ready to lead off the parade. Anna's older sister, Melissa, came up to them. She said that hundreds of people were standing along School Street and Main Street to watch the parade. She held up the contribution box. "I have to empty it," Melissa said. "It's stuffed to the top, and more people want to contribute! They all loved Winston."

"Good work," said Pam.

"Where's Ms. Wiggins?" asked Anna.

"In front of Town Hall," Melissa said.

The band struck up a marching song. The festival organizer signaled to Pam and Lulu to start the parade. They directed their ponies onto School Street. Mr. Olson told Acorn to walk on and he did.

Acorn held his head high, his ears were forward, and he walked with a beautiful stride. The cart seemed to glide behind him. People cheered. Anna turned to her right and left and smiled at her neighbors.

Anna saw Ms. Wiggins in front of Town Hall with Melissa. Ms. Wiggins was surprised to see Lightning and Snow White in the parade. Then she saw Acorn pulling the cart. She waved and smiled to Anna. Anna waved back. When Lulu and Pam reached Town Hall, they stopped their ponies. Mr. Olson halted Acorn. Anna motioned for Ms. Wiggins to come over.

"Want to climb aboard?" Mr. Olson asked Ms. Wiggins. She nodded. Mr. Olson told Melissa to hold Acorn by the bridle. Then he handed the reins and whip to Anna and stepped out of the cart. Ms. Wiggins climbed in next to Anna. The band began a new song. The festival organizer signaled Lulu and Pam to ride on. Anna held the lines out for Ms. Wiggins, but she shook her head no. "You drive, Anna," she said. "It's your turn. Yours and Acorn's."

Anna and Ms. Wiggins were smiling. But they both had tears in their eyes.

The parade went around the Town

Green, up School Street, and ended in the parking lot. Anna and Ms. Wiggins climbed out of the cart. There was still one surprise that Ms. Wiggins didn't know about.

"Look at the back of the cart," Anna told Ms. Wiggins. Anna held Acorn by the bridle while Ms. Wiggins walked behind the cart. She read the sign aloud.

Winston. 30 Years.
Goodbye to a Wonderful Pony.

A crowd gathered around the pony and cart. "Is this pony taking Winston's place in the parade?" someone asked.

"Yes, he is," said Ms. Wiggins.

"What's his name?" another person asked.

"His name is Acorn," answered Anna. She put her hand on Acorn's mane. "Winston and Acorn were friends."

"Hooray for Acorn!" someone shouted.

People clapped. Anna gave Acorn a great big hug. "You did it, Acorn," she told him. "You did it."

Dear Reader:

I am having a lot of fun researching and writing books about the Pony Pals. I've met many interesting kids and adults who love ponies. And I've visited some wonderful ponies at homes, farms, and riding schools.

Before writing Pony Pals I wrote fourteen novels for children and young adults. Four of these were honored by Children's Choice Awards.

I live in Sharon, Connecticut, with my husband, Lee, and our dog, Willie. Our daughter is all grown up and has her own apartment in New York City.

Besides writing novels I like to draw, paint, garden, and swim. I didn't have a pony when I was growing up, but I have always loved them and dreamt about riding. Now I take riding lessons on a horse named Saz.

I like reading and writing about ponies as much as I do riding. Which proves to me that you don't have to ride a pony to love them. And you certainly don't need a pony to be a Pony Pal.

Happy Reading,

Jeanne Betancourt

PONY PALS

Do you love ponies?

Be a Pony Pal!

Anna, Pam, and Lulu want you to join them
on adventures with their favorite ponies!

Order now and you get a free pony portrait bookmark
and two collecting cards in all the books—for you *and*
your pony pal!

❑ BBC48583-0	#1	I Want a Pony	$2.95
❑ BBC48584-9	#2	A Pony for Keeps	$2.99
❑ BBC48585-7	#3	A Pony in Trouble	$2.99
❑ BBC48586-5	#4	Give Me Back My Pony	$2.99
❑ BBC25244-5	#5	Pony to the Rescue	$2.99
❑ BBC25245-3	#6	Too Many Ponies	$2.99
❑ BBC54338-5	#7	Runaway Pony	$2.99

Available wherever you buy books, or use this order form.

Send orders to Scholastic Inc., P.O. Box 7500, 2931 East McCarty Street,
Jefferson City, MO 65102.

Please send me the books I have checked above. I am enclosing $_____ (please add
$2.00 to cover shipping and handling). Send check or money order — no cash or
C.O.D.s please.

Please allow four to six weeks for delivery. Offer good in the U.S.A. only. Sorry,
mail orders are not available to residents in Canada. Prices subject to change.

Name_____Birthdate ____/____/____
          First   Last   M / D / Y

Address_____

City_____State_____Zip_____

Telephone (   ) _____ ❑ Boy ❑ Girl

Where did you buy this book? ❑ Bookstore ❑ Book Fair ❑ Book Club ❑ Other

LITTLE  APPLE®

There are fun times ahead with kids just like you in Little Apple books! Once you take a bite out of a Little Apple—you'll want to read more!

❏ NA42833-0	**Catwings** Ursula K. LeGuin	$2.95
❏ NA42832-2	**Catwings Return** Ursula K. LeGuin	$2.95
❏ NA41821-1	**Class Clown** Johanna Hurwitz	$2.75
❏ NA43868-9	**The Haunting of Grade Three** Grace Maccarone	$2.75
❏ NA40966-2	**Rent A Third Grader** B.B. Hiller	$2.99
❏ NA41944-7	**The Return of the Third Grade Ghost Hunters** Grace Maccarone	$2.75
❏ NA44477-8	**Santa Claus Doesn't Mop Floors** Debra Dadey and Marcia Thornton Jones	$2.99
❏ NA42031-3	**Teacher's Pet** Johanna Hurwitz	$2.99
❏ NA43411-X	**Vampires Don't Wear Polka Dots** Debra Dadey and Marcia Thornton Jones	$2.99
❏ NA44061-6	**Werewolves Don't Go to Summer Camp** Debra Dadey and Marcia Thornton Jones	$2.99

Available wherever you buy books...or use the coupon below.

THE *Berenstain* BEAR® SCOUTS

by Stan & Jan Berenstain

Join Scouts Brother, Sister, Fred, and Lizzy as they defend the weak, catch the crooked, joust against the unjust, and rally against rottenness of all kinds!

Collect all the books in this great new series!

Don't miss the Berenstain Bear Scouts' first two exciting adventures!

☐ BBF60380-9 **The Berenstain Bear Scouts and the Humongous Pumpkin** $2.99

☐ BBF60379-5 **The Berenstain Bear Scouts in Giant Bat Cave** $2.99

© 1995 Berenstain Enterprises, Inc.
Available wherever you buy books or use this order form.

- -

Send orders to:
Scholastic Inc., P.O. Box 7502, 2931 East McCarty Street, Jefferson City, MO 65102-7500

Please send me the books I have checked above. I am enclosing $———— (please add $2.00 to cover shipping and handling). Send check or money order — no cash or C.O.D.s please.

Name _____ Birthdate __/__/__
                                                                 M D Y

Address _____

City _____ State _____ Zip _____

Please allow four to six weeks for delivery. Offer good in U.S.A. only. Sorry, mail orders are not available to residents of Canada. Prices subject to change.

BBR6